WARNING!

Scaredy Squirrel insists that everyone put on No.65 sunscreen before reading this book.

For Sergio, Nelson and Pablo, who bravely helped us build our very own beach getaway

Text and illustrations © 2008 Mélanie Watt

This edition is only available for distribution through the school market by Scholastic Book Fairs and Scholastic Canada Ltd.

ISBN 978-1-55453-783-9

CM 09 0 9 8 7 6 5 4 3 2 1
CM PA 11 0 9 8 7 6 5 4 3 2 1

Kids Can Press acknowledges the financial support of the Government of Ontario, through the Ontario Media Development Corporation's Ontario Book Initiative; the Ontario Arts Council; the Canada Council for the Arts; and the Government of Canada, through the BPIDP, for our publishing activity.

Published in Canada by
Kids Can Press Ltd.
25 Dockside Drive
Toronto, ON M5A 0B5

Published in the U.S. by
Kids Can Press Ltd.
2250 Military Road
Tonawanda, NY 14150

www.kidscanpress.com

The artwork in this book was rendered digitally in Photoshop.
The text is set in Potato Cut.

Edited by Tara Walker
Designed by Mélanie Watt and Karen Powers

The hardcover edition of this book is smyth sewn casebound.
The paperback edition of this book is limp sewn with a drawn-on cover.
Manufactured in Tseung Kwan O, Kowloon, Hong Kong, China, in 3/2011 by Paramount Printing Co. Ltd.

CM 08 0 9 8 7 6 5

LIBRARY AND ARCHIVES CANADA CATALOGUING IN PUBLICATION

Watt, Mélanie, 1975–
    Scaredy Squirrel at the beach / Mélanie Watt.

ISBN 978-1-55453-225-4

I. Title.

PS8645.A8845282 2007   jC813'.6   C2007-904347-X

Kids Can Press is a  Entertainment company

Scaredy Squirrel

at the beach

by Mélanie Watt

KIDS CAN PRESS

TAKE A BEACH VACATION!

Scaredy Squirrel never goes to the beach. He'd rather vacation at home alone where it's safe than risk being surrounded by the wrong crowd.

A few crowds Scaredy Squirrel wouldn't want to be caught in the middle of:

flocks of seagulls

tribes of jellyfish

herds of sea monsters

packs of pirates

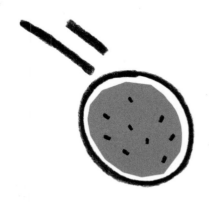

tons of falling coconuts

mobs of lobsters

So he's perfectly happy to build his very own private beach.

Scaredy Squirrel's Guide to Building a Safe Beach

What you need to get started:

paper and crayons

1 stick

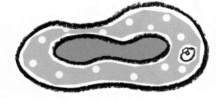

1 inflatable pool

1 flashlight

1 bag of kitty litter

1 plastic flamingo

1. Draw beach "scenery."

2. Use stick to hold upright.

3. Cover ground with "sand."

4. Inflate "ocean."

5. Turn on "sunlight."

6. Install beach "wildlife"...

And ENJOY!

TOCK
TOCK
TOCK

NO GERMS!

It looks like a beach and feels like a beach, but it doesn't sound like one. Scaredy Squirrel notices something's missing: the soothing sound of the ocean!

THE SOLUTION:
Make a quick trip to the REAL beach and find a seashell that fits the description below.

SEASHELL
(Quality and Performance Chart)

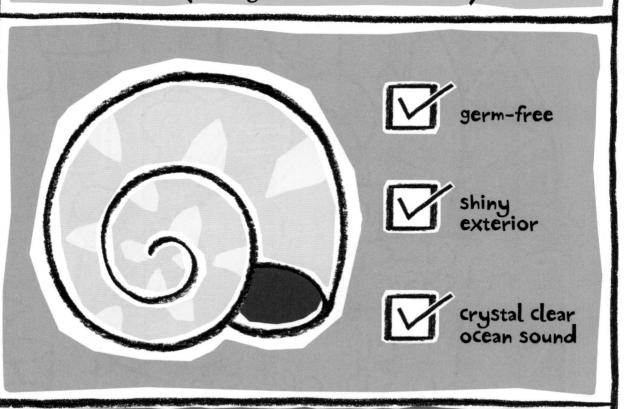

- ☑ germ-free
- ☑ shiny exterior
- ☑ crystal clear ocean sound

RED ALERT! Seashell must NOT, I repeat, NOT be occupied!

But traveling to the REAL beach requires careful planning.

First, get a passport.

NO GERMS!

SUBJECT HAS NEVER TRAVELED

S///000//SOS//UNKNOWN)))

—PASSPORT—

Family: rodent
Type: flying squirrel
First name: Scaredy
Middle name: Orville
Last name: Squirrel
Initials: S.O.S.
Place of birth: nut tree

Second, draw a map ...

BEACH MAP

(MISSION: Operation Seashell)

7:00 a.m.: Enter box and wait
(don't forget passport)

7:30 a.m.: Get picked up by mail truck
(verify passport)

8:42 a.m.: Arrive at beach and wait until
the coast is clear
(don't lose passport)

11:42 a.m.: Exit box and find seashell
(hold passport)

1:49 p.m.: Enter box and wait for pick-up
(check passport)

6:00 p.m.: Get delivered back to nut tree
(put away passport)

Caution: falling coconuts have a mind of their own — they can knock you out without warning.

Important: sea monsters are camera shy, so keep camera close by.

AHOY MATEY! Watch fer pirates. AARRR! They'll make ye walk the plank!

X Seashell should be here.

Stay away from tribes of jellyfish: you'll be stung by how sneaky they can be.

Never trust a mob of lobsters: they are a pinch territorial and are eager to snap.

Careful: birds of a feather flock together. Seagulls can drop by at any time!

N
W   E
S

And last but not least, travel light and dress accordingly. ➡

SCAREDY'S BEACHWEAR

This squirrel is a trained professional. Don't try this at home!

Exhibit A:
Protective headgear for falling coconuts

Exhibit B:
Protective eye patch to fool pirates

Exhibit C:
Protective floatation device to prevent sinking

Exhibit D:
Protective camera to discourage sea monsters

Exhibit E:
Protective compass to avoid getting lost

Exhibit I:
Protective french fry to distract seagulls

Exhibit H:
Protective oven mitts to block germs

Exhibit G:
Protective rubber band to tame lobsters

Exhibit F:
Protective footgear to shield from jellyfish

Remember, if all else fails, play dead and send an SOS!

The next morning, as planned, Scaredy Squirrel jumps into the box.

At 7:30 a.m. he gets picked up. They drive ...

... and drive.

WELCOME TO THE BEACH!

At 8:42 a.m. Scaredy gets dropped off and waits ... and waits.

PEOPLE were NOT part of the Plan!

Scaredy Squirrel panics and ...

PLAYS DEAD.

30 minutes later

1 hour later

2 hours later

Finally Scaredy Squirrel realizes that the perfect seashell is right under his nose.

Surrounded by friendly people, he decides to join the crowd.

SURF'S UP!

Scaredy Squirrel builds sand castles ...

takes pictures ...

floats around in the ocean ...

and sunbathes with the others.

He forgets all about the flocks of seagulls, tribes of jellyfish, herds of sea monsters, packs of pirates, tons of falling coconuts and mobs of lobsters.

He's glad to be part of the crowd!

Back home, after a day of fun in the sun, Scaredy Squirrel's inspired to make one more important addition to his own beach ...

garden gnomes

P.S. As for Scaredy's next visit to the beach, it might be sooner than he thinks ...

RED ALERT!